Freedom Soup

Tami Charles
illustrated by Jacqueline Alcántara

CANDLEWICK PRESS

Today is New Year's Day. This year, I get to help make Freedom Soup. Ti Gran says I've got a heart made for cooking, and it's time I learn how.

Outside, snow is piling, cottony-thick. Inside, warm, sweet air flows.

Haitian kompa pours through the speakers. The shake-shake of maracas vibrates down to my toes.

Ti Gran's feet tap-tap to the rhythm.

We pause our dancing, and Ti Gran says, "First, Belle, is the epis."

She places the pilon between my knees.

Click! Clack!   *Click! Clack!*

Together, we mash the garlicky herbs to the kompa beat.
Then we add it to our meat and let it rest.

"Next is your favorite —"

"The pumpkin?"

Ti Gran smiles and pulls it out of the boiling water. Ribbons of steam dance up to the ceiling.

She lets me peel the pumpkin. The skin melts off like butter.

Then Ti Gran browns the meat in a new pot and gathers the rest of the ingredients: pumpkin, herbs, potatoes, carrots, cabbage, and celery.

"Your turn," she says.

One by one, I slide the ingredients into the bubbling liquid.
The pumpkiny-garlic smell swirls all around us.

"Know why they call it Freedom Soup?" Ti Gran asks.

"Because it's free?"

It's the same answer I always give. Ti Gran laughs her loud, belly-deep laugh.

"Oh, Belle. Nothing in this world is free, not even freedom."

She begins to tell a story, the same one she tells every year. A story of the place she was born: Haiti.

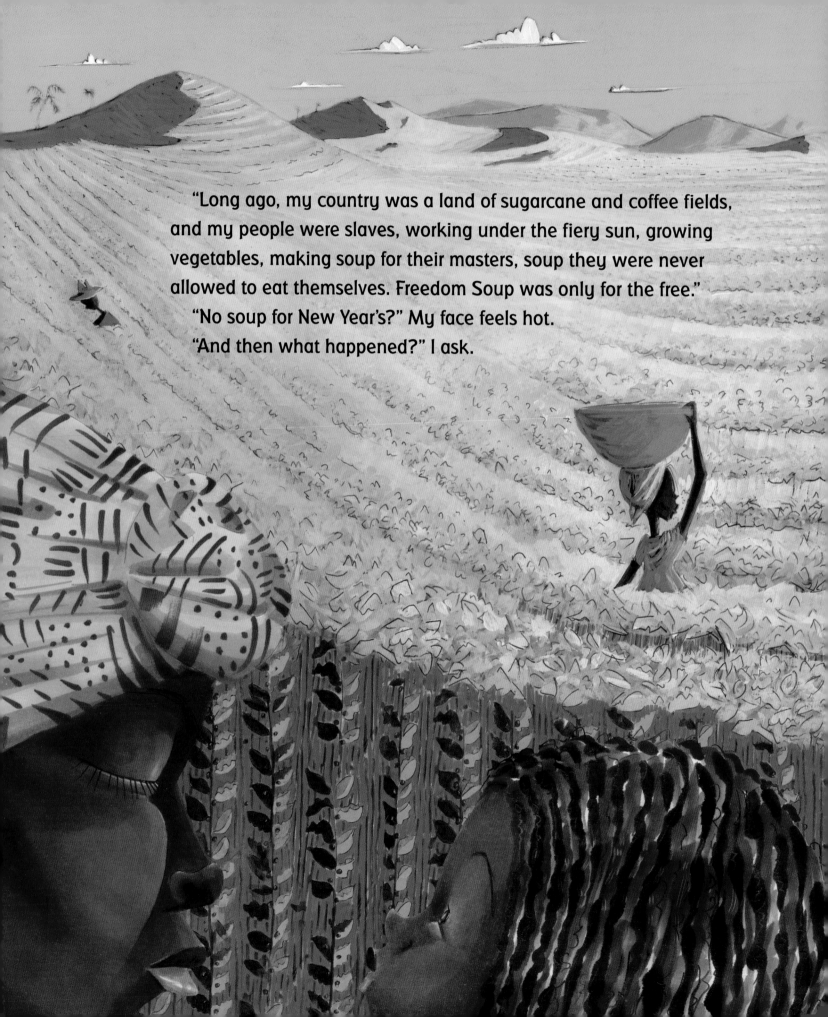

"Long ago, my country was a land of sugarcane and coffee fields, and my people were slaves, working under the fiery sun, growing vegetables, making soup for their masters, soup they were never allowed to eat themselves. Freedom Soup was only for the free."

"No soup for New Year's?" My face feels hot.

"And then what happened?" I ask.

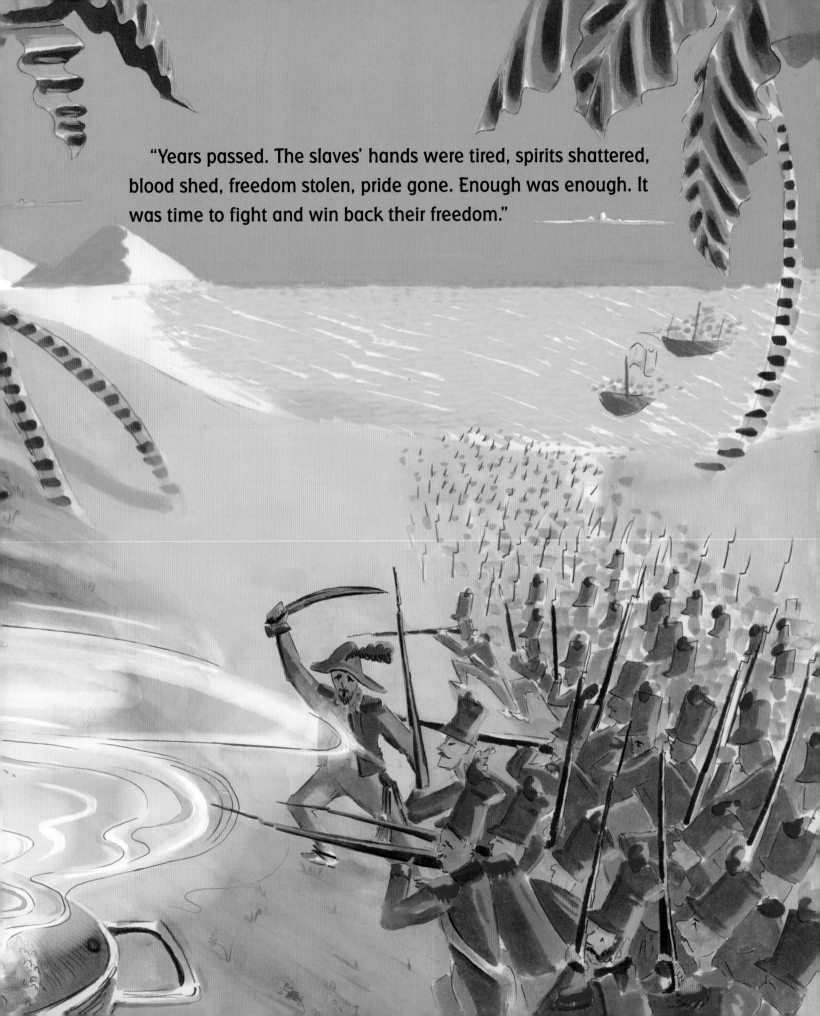

"Years passed. The slaves' hands were tired, spirits shattered, blood shed, freedom stolen, pride gone. Enough was enough. It was time to fight and win back their freedom."

The trumpet blares.
"I hear it, Ti Gran! The revolution is here!"

The kompa beat drums through my skin.
I see them — the fire dancing in their eyes as they fight to take
back what's theirs.

I see the colors of freedom: the tan streets of Port-au-Prince,
covered in broken black chains, kettles of hot yellow soup,
a sweet pumpkiny-garlic aroma filling the air.
I see Ti Gran's people. My people.
Eating soup to celebrate the end of slavery.
Eating soup to celebrate the start of freedom.

We clap our hands and sing to the sky,
"Haiti is free!
Freedom Soup for everyone!"

Ti Gran lowers the flame while I throw in the pasta.
"My grandmother taught this tradition to my manman, who taught it to me. I taught it to your mother . . ."
"And I'll teach my children one day?"

Ti Gran's dark-sky eyes smile as we rest in the living room and she pulls me in real close.
"And they'll share it with everyone who will come after."

The pumpkiny-garlic smell scents the air as cousins, uncles,
and aunts arrive and dance.
   We share stories of Ti Gran's faraway island, and taste freedom
again . . . and again . . . and again . . .

"What a lovely soup you made, Belle," they say.
I puff out my shoulders wider than the Haitian mountains,
stand so tall I can almost touch the moon.

All around, just like my family, people gather and share. In our house, we celebrate until the last drop of soup is gone,
    gone,
        gone!

FREEDOM SOUP

There are lots of ways to make this soup. Ingredients vary by household and also by region of Haiti. It can be cooked with any type of meat. My personal favorites are beef, chicken, and turkey. Freedom Soup made with seafood is also a delicious option! Or you can leave out the meat altogether and make a vegetarian version.

Here, I've created an easy, no-fuss, kid-friendly recipe. Traditional Freedom Soup can include more vegetables and often uses *joumou,* calabaza squash. You'll notice that my recipe is slightly different from the one Belle makes. It uses frozen butternut squash, which can be easier to find in the market than pumpkin.

EPIS

Epis is a common marinade used with meats and to flavor many Haitian dishes.

INGREDIENTS

3 scallions, coarsely chopped
3 garlic cloves
2 bell peppers (red and/or green),
    seeds removed, coarsely chopped
5 sprigs of thyme
$1/2$ cup chopped cilantro
$1/2$ cup chopped parsley
2 celery stalks, coarsely chopped
$1/4$ cup olive oil
$1/2$ cup lime juice
1 teaspoon vinegar

DIRECTIONS

1. Blend all the ingredients in a blender, or mash them using a pilon (mortar and pestle).

2. Pour over the meat you will use for the soup.

3. Marinate for up to 24 hours.

SOUP

INGREDIENTS

2 pounds of your preferred marinated meat
2 tablespoons olive oil
8 cups stock (beef, chicken, or vegetable)
2 packages frozen butternut squash
1 Scotch bonnet pepper (optional)
$1/2$ teaspoon dried thyme
2 tablespoons chopped parsley
2 tablespoons chopped cilantro
1 large potato, peeled and cut into $1 1/2$-inch pieces
    (could substitute with malanga or use both)
2 carrots, cut into $1 1/2$-inch pieces
2 stalks celery, cut into $1 1/2$-inch pieces
$1/2$ small green cabbage, cored and cut into $1 1/2$-inch pieces
1 handful of spaghetti, broken in half

DIRECTIONS

1. In a large soup pot, brown the meat in the olive oil.

2. Add the stock, squash, and Scotch bonnet pepper. Boil until the meat reaches your desired level of tenderness.

3. Add the thyme, parsley, cilantro, and potato to the pot. Continue boiling for approximately 15 minutes.

4. Add the carrots, celery, and cabbage. Reduce heat, and simmer for approximately 25 minutes, or until tender.

5. Stir occasionally until the soup thickens. Add the spaghetti and cook according to package directions.

6. Don't forget to remove the Scotch bonnet pepper!

7. Add salt and pepper, to taste.

Bon appétit!

AUTHOR'S NOTE

My husband's late grandmother, Ti Gran, gave me my first bowl of Freedom Soup, also known as Soup Joumou. As soon as I tasted it, I knew there had to be a story behind the flavors of pride, victory, and joy. Ti Gran was a feisty yet gentle soul who taught me the history of the soup.

Slavery began on the island of Haiti as early as 1492, with the arrival of Christopher Columbus. Slavery is the practice of forcing someone to work without pay. Initially, the indigenous people of Haiti, the Taíno, were forced into slavery. By 1514, Africans were being brought to the island to work as slaves after the Taíno population was largely exterminated due to harsh treatment and sicknesses brought by European colonists. Fast forward to 1791. This was the start of the Haitian Revolution, the most successful slave rebellion in the Western Hemisphere. Former slave Toussaint L'Ouverture would emerge as the leader of this movement. The revolution lasted for twelve years. Finally, in 1803, slavery was abolished in Haiti and the island nation claimed its independence from France. On January 1, 1804, Haiti acknowledged this accomplishment. Today, Haitian Independence Day is celebrated among families all over the world. Freedom Soup is a key element in these celebrations.

As parents, it's important for my husband and me to carry on this tradition with our son, Christopher. Every New Year's Day, I make Freedom Soup with my son while teaching him a bit of history about the island that his father's people come from.

It's been several years since Ti Gran left us, and I continue to be thankful for the lessons she taught me: that freedom comes at a price, that the price you pay is the work you put in, and that the ultimate reward is tasting the sweet freedom that you craved all along. This book is an homage to Ti Gran and to the bravery of the Haitian people, who have endured so much, in fighting their revolution, in the face of an earthquake, and in the face of continual oppression. Through all of this, the spirit of the Haitian people continues to rise.

L'union fait la force!
Unity makes strength!